I0588522

VOLUME FIVE

SHORT BITS

FIVE ORIGINAL SCIENCE FICTION & FANTASY STORIES

BELINDA CRAWFORD

HENDRIX & FAUST
PUBLISHERS

Published by Hendrix & Faust, Publishers in 2025
Text copyright © Belinda Crawford 2025

www.belindacrawford.com

ISBN: 978-0-6459318-3-9 (ebook)
ISBN: 978-0-6459318-4-6 (paperback)

All rights reserved. No part of this book may be reproduced or transmitted by any person or entity, including internet search engines or retailers, in any form or by any means, electronic or mechanical, including photocopying (except under the statutory exceptions provisions of the *Australian Copyright Act 1968*), recording, scanning or by any information storage and retrieval system without the prior written permission of the publisher.

NO AI TRAINING: Without in any way limiting the author's [and publisher's] exclusive rights under copyright, any use of this publication to "train" generative artificial intelligence (AI) technologies to generate text is expressly prohibited. The author reserves all rights to license uses of this work for generative AI training and development of machine learning language models.

This is a work of fiction. Names, characters, businesses, places, events, locales, and incidents are either the products of the author's imagination or used in a fictitious manner. Any resemblance to actual persons, living or dead, or actual events is purely coincidental.

PRINTED AND BOUND BY INGRAMSPARK.
Australia: Ingram Content Group AU Pty Ltd, Melbourne, Victoria. US: Lightning Source LLC, La Vergne, Tennessee / Allentown, Pennsylvania / Jackson, Tennessee, United States. UK: Lightning Source UK Ltd, Milton Keynes, United Kingdom. Europe: Lightning Source UK Ltd, with facilities in Germany, France, and Spain.

The authorized representative in the European Economic Area is Lightning Source France, 1 Av. Johannes Gutenberg, 78310 Maurepas, France. compliance@lightningsource.fr

Books by Belinda Crawford

The Hero Rebellion
(Hunter)
Hero
(Race)
Riven
Regan

The Echo
Cold Between Stars
Dark Between Oceans
Echo Between Worlds
(Brother)

Gamer

Demons & Battleskirts
Volume 1

Short Bits
Short Bits Collected Edition 1
(collecting volumes 1–4)

CONTENTS

Introduction 7

So Long & Thanks for all the Diamonds 9

A Country Event 31

The Polar Bear 51

Bug Hunt 63

The Deli 85

INTRODUCTION

Where *Short Bits, Volume 4* was a milestone celebrating two years since I started these short story collections, this fifth volume is a different kind of milestone. One of completion.

All of the stories in *Short Bits 5* have languished in various states of in-progress for quite a while. *The Deli* takes the crown for the longest; both the story and the name "Short Bits" originate from my time working in a delicatessen. My experience working behind the counter is responsible for the former, while bacon, specifically short cut bacon, takes out the honours for the latter.

So Long & Thanks for All the Diamonds has been staring me down for a couple of years now (more on that in the story's introduction), a sassy blonde daring me to tell her tale. *A Country Event* began life as a writing exercise that refused to stay contained, and the others have been hanging around my head, banging on the walls for just as long.

As always, I'm keep track of stories that resonate most with readers, so if any of these grab you, let me know. Your favourite may just make it to the top of my To-Write list.

Happy reading,
Belinda

So Long,

& THANKS FOR ALL THE DIAMONDS

INTRODUCTION

So Long & Thanks for All the Diamonds was inspired by a book cover.

Way back when, I used to design things for a living, book covers included. One day while I was noodling around in Photoshop, I created a cover featuring a bombshell blonde in the driver's seat of a convertible, looking over her shoulder. It had a very 1940s noir vibe, right down to the sepia tones and the bombshell's elbow-length gloves.

Every book needs a title, so I gave it one, *this* one. Don't ask me what inspired me to riff off Douglas Adams, I've never really been much of a fan, but the name stuck and... here it is. A story inspired by a book cover. It seems kinda backwards, but that's inspiration for you.

SO LONG & THANKS FOR ALL THE DIAMONDS

The dame sat across from him, blonde hair in the kinda waves that rolled off the beach in a bob that flirted with one side of her jaw. The other side was tucked behind her ear, showing off a waterfall of nano-diamonds hanging from an ivory lobe. She sat in the plain metal chair like she was in a nightclub, not an interrogation room, leaning back and smiling at him as if she knew something.

Not that that was a surprise. He *knew* she knew something, and a whole lot more than something if he had to bet, and he was a betting man. A betting man with a badge, even if it was a little stained these days, smoky around the edges.

She looked like she appreciated smoky, maybe even charred. Hell, Ms Lorelei Lee—aged fifty-seven and still looking like she was barely thirty, resident of New Sydney on an extended travel visa to Old Syd—probably spit and roasted cops in her palatial Luna Major mansion just for fun. Same way she lifted Old Man Arend's diamonds.

Just for fun.

Fuck knew she didn't need the cash.

There'd probably be the same look in her big dark eyes as she stoked the fire under the cops, the same arch to her winged brows—the kinda dark brown that didn't come natural to that platinum hair—the same kick to the dark, engine-red lips. Waiting. Knowing.

Daring.

He drummed his fingers on the table – tattoos crawling over the joints, blunt and worn at the tips, still not quite thawed from the night spent staked outside the Hyatt Classic in his old Jeep, waiting for the dame to show up in the midst of an Old Syd ice-snap. The table was the same metal as the chairs, light and cold and cheap, had the same sensors in it too—biological and electronic—picking up everything from the dame's perspiration rate to the signals pinging the comm implanted behind her left ear, the one without the diamond waterfall.

She tilted her head and those ocean curls moved with her, waterfall sparkling as it spilled over her shoulder, bared to the cleavage by the gold sequinned sheath she called a dress.

Interrogation lights were harsh, the kinda blue-white daylight that leeched colour from everything and turned shadows into ink stains, and yet it glided over the dame like the small, square room was a stage and she the star in her strapless, floor-length gown.

Neat trick.

He stopped drumming his fingers. 'Where were you at eleven-fifteen, Ms Lee?'

Her smile widened. 'Don't you already know, detective?' She had a voice like honey, smooth and thick, unlike his; rough as the smog he sucked down every morning like it was mama's milk.

'I think you were in the vault hidden behind Old Man Arend's suits, Ms Lee, helping yourself to that diamond and sapphire necklace he likes to wear to the opera.'

She tilted her head the other way, the wave and the waterfall following. 'Really? I don't believe I've seen it.'

'It's hard to miss, Ms Lee, got a sapphire pendant bigger 'an an Easter egg.' He held his scarred, meaty fist up for comparison. 'Just about bends the old man in half it does.'

She propped that round chin on a gloved fist and smiled at him. A little smile, warmth kicking up the edges of those red, red lips. 'Really?' she said. 'I didn't know. How fascinating, but then we all make sacrifices for the things we love.'

'And what do you love, Ms Lee?'

'Diamonds,' she said.

'What about the late Mr Lee?'

'He didn't love diamonds, more of a leg man.'

'Did you love him, ma'am?'

She settled her cheek on her palm and he swore, for a moment, her eyes glittered like the rocks he'd bet ten-to-nine she'd lifted while the Old Man and his guests were busy quaffing century-old brandy.

Again, those lips smiled. 'I loved his diamonds.' She sat back, a smooth quick motion that scraped the chair across the old floor—concrete, the better to hose the piss and vomit down the drain in the middle—and flipped one long, long leg over the other. It was done in a moment, barely enough time for his heart to ride up a pitch or the locks on the chair arms to side into place and hold her still. 'He loved my legs.'

He was sure Mr Lee had. They were nice legs, the long slit in the dress's sleek skirt doing its job, parting over the one on display, the gold a perfect foil for the sleek calf and trim ankle. Those legs were an investment, he was sure, time and money spent in equal measure, and he'd bet again she didn't just use 'em for dancing.

He echoed her posture, but slower, the old metal chair groaning a little under his weight. His legs didn't cross so easy—old scars pulling—but he got his ankle across his knee, ignoring the muddy smear it left on his pant leg. The jeans had seen worse, like his face.

'Doesn't seem like much of a basis for marriage, Ms Lee.'

'We both got what we wanted.' She tilted her head, spilling the platinum wave to the other side. 'Is this really what you want to ask me, Detective?'

He drummed his fingers on the table, a steady *rat tat tat*. 'Just making conversation.'

Silence. Stretching.

She continued to smile at him, bouncing her foot, just a little, never breaking eye contact.

Most folk he sat down in that chair tried the same – big men, meaner women, smart and stupid and the whole rainbow in between. He had that kind of face; rough, craggy, caverns for eyes, cliffs for cheekbones, worn and weathered just like the whiskey beard and the moustache. The kinda face that didn't belong on a cop, just like the tats and the thick gold rings on his fingers.

But then, he'd never been a terribly good cop.

Most people avoided his gaze, hid behind fringes or coughs, but not this dame.

'So,' he said, just to break the silence. Enough of it to hear the cyclers pushing air through the vents and the mouse that maintenance never caught.

She arched a thick brown brow. 'So,' she echoed.

'Eleven fifteen, Ms Lee. Where were you?'

He foot bounced, the diamond-studded dragon coiling over her arch drinking the interrogation lights. 'Powdering my nose.'

'In Old Man Arend's vault?'

Another bounce, another flash. 'I've never had the pleasure.'

He didn't twitch, didn't change his breathing when his heart spiked. A little victory pulsing through his veins. 'You sure?'

Her cheek went back to her gloved hand. 'Positive.'

'Then why'd we find your prints inside the vault, Ms Lee?'

'Are you sure they were mine?'

'Positive,' he said again.

'Hmm.' Her foot never lost its rhythm. 'Maybe you should check them again.'

'We already have, Ms Lee. Three times. Maybe you want to change your story?'

She shook her head, platinum waves brushing her cheeks, the nano-diamonds brushing against her long throat. 'No, I'm quite happy with the one I have.'

'It's grand larceny, Ms Lee. That's twenty-five years in old Long Bay.'

'Hmm.' Amusement warmed her eyes.

'Perhaps you want to call your lawyer.'

'Perhaps I don't.'

'It's a serious charge.'

Her eyes glittered, and those lips twitched. 'You look like a serious man.'

Unease trailed greasy fingers over his scalp. Something wasn't right, suspects didn't act like the dame; the guilty ones twitted and fizzed, no matter how well they lied, and the innocent ones were earnest or angry or sad. The dame was none of those things.

Another tap on the desk, not his previous drumming but a quick *rat rat*. The nano-tech in the metal didn't hum, but he imagined it did, couldn't quite get the thought out, much the same as he clung to his cigars and ancient Jeep. Hell, he'd only submitted to the corneal implant, and only in the one eye because it was the only way he could stay a cop. Paranoia, his ex had called it, the belief that the tech was gonna get him one day. Still, the implant had its uses, like connection to the robbery squad's AI—REX—and the data it popped over his eyeball.

Heartbeat, respiration, perspiration and vocal stress overlaying the engine-red lips and platinum bob.

// No subversive tech detected, REX said. *All readings suggest Ms Lee is innocent. Analysis recommends you look for a different suspect, Detective.*

Yeah, he'd believe that when he found the diamonds, and probably not even then. There was something about the woman, the way the dragon snaked around her ankle, the earring played with her collarbone.

'How'd you get from the second floor to the vault, Ms Lee?'

Her head tilted. 'Who says I did, Detective?'

'Your fingerprint, in the vault. Which you say you've never been in.'

'Is that all you have then? My fingerprint?'

'You have a history, ma'am.' He *rat ratted* the table and

information scrolled over his eye. 'Things have a habit of going missing when you're around.'

She straightened in the chair, just a little. The movement slight enough most wouldn't see it.

Nervous?

'Do they? What kind of things?'

'Diamonds, Ms Lee. Diamonds go missing when you're around.'

A laugh. On his screen, vocal stress spiked. 'Well, people do like to give me things.'

'Do they also like to file police reports after?'

'Their wives perhaps.' She considered a moment. 'Husbands too, I guess.'

'Is that what happened to the Beekman's necklace last April?'

'Frannie's necklace? The one with the—' She gestured to her neck '—diamond snake? Although, she did try to convince me it was a dragon.'

'That's the one.'

She shook her head. 'I didn't have the honour.'

'Really? File photos suggest it looks a lot like the dragon on your shoes.' He pointed to the diamonds winking over her arch.

The dame laughed. 'These old things? They're not diamonds, detective, and certainly not Frannie's little…' She gestured to her throat again. '…snake.'

'Aren't they?'

'No, but then your AI should have told you that the moment I walked into the department.'

// She is correct, Sergeant. The gems on Ms Lee's shoes are high-grade nano-diamonds, manufactured by Lab Arendis.

He rubbed the spot behind his ear. Even after fifteen years, he still hadn't gotten use to the way the comm made his skin buzz.

// Internal systems have detected a slight vibration coming from Ms Lee's diamonds that is causing some inter— int—

A screech—banshees wailing to claws on a blackboard—

rammed electricity through his eardrums, down his spine. Took muscle and tendon hostage, locking him to the chair, sure as the thick metallic cuffs snapping out of the arms and over his wrists, except for the brief moment where he tried to jerk upright. He succeeded only in toppling, chair and all to the floor.

On his eyeball, light. A sharp, hideous flicker, the banshees' nails grinding through the wet stuff to leave marks on the inside of his skull. Pain pulled his lips from his teeth, set his spine rigid and had nausea twisting his gut. A whine pushed past clenched teeth, and even his beard hurt, every follicle an icy spear ripping his face.

Through it all, he saw the dame, a divine vision superimposed over the pain. Watched in agonising slow-motion as she uncrossed her legs, the diamond-studded dragons holding her stilettos, another dagger to his eyeball. She stood, unfolding from her metal throne, a queen with her crown not nestled in her platinum waves but trailing over her smooth, bare shoulder, the nano-diamonds in her earring shifting, folding, growing. A sparkling river tracing the line of her throat, all the way over her chest, connecting with other sparks, threads in her gold sequinned dress.

Impossible to tell how far the river went, if it cascaded all the way to her shoes, the dragon stilettos, not with the desk between them, not with the light and sound show holding him hostage.

On his eyeball, REX regained some function, not enough to trigger his internal chem-pharm, but enough to clear the screech from his ear and pause the vomit-inducing light show.

// Mainframe bree— bree— breech. Internal hack detected. Estimated time to security reboot… eighteen minutes. And then. *//* *Hang in there, Sergeant.*

Her stilettos clacked on the concrete, the dragons climbing her feet, glinting as they twisted around her ankles.

The dame knelt beside him, skirt splitting over her knee. With his cheek plastered to the cold floor, he could appreciate the pale expanse of smooth white skin stretched over lean muscle, the way the dress cinched in at her waist, emphasising the swell of her hips under the gold.

The smile never left her face, neither her dark-copper eyes or her engine-red lips, as she reached down and smoothed the ends of his 'tash either side of his mouth. She gave his cheek a pat before she traced her hand over his shoulder, down his arm and picked up his hand.

The restraint opened at her touch, the metal clattering against the concrete but there was no strength in him to resist, nothing but the teeth-clenching nausea.

She spread his fingers and pressed his hand, palm and all to her ribs. The gold sequins flashed and shivered, and she let him go, placing his hand back on the cold chair arm, the restraint clicking back into place.

'It'll be over soon,' she said, before she rose and sashayed out the door.

◊

Old Man Arend's diamond necklace, complete with the Easter Egg sapphire wasn't missing, it was in the leacher's body. The Lab Arendis prototype an expensive show of light, nanotech and manufactured carbon few could appreciate. But she could, and she did. Frequently.

The showmanship was one thing, the pained frown between his eyes—small, but not too small—the slight grimace pulling at his smile, the way his left hand—wrinkled and weighed with gold— found its way to his back, almost unconsciously as if that big ol' sapphire pained him.

Perfect. Even she'd been fooled. At first.

But as much as beautiful an act this was… She shivered as she waltzed through the robbery division, past the police officers and detectives passed out on the rough charcoal carpet, the desks, half-propped against walls and sagging against doorframes, every single one held captive to the lights dancing in their ocular implants.

As beautiful as Old Man's Arend's performance was, it was nothing to his technology.

She shivered again. Beautiful.

Diamonds might have been a girl's best friend last century but in this one, it was the kind of tech that made something out of nothing.

The man had always had a way about him, right up until he decided he wanted his way with her. And that... well, that required a little lesson.

The old man's vault was for show, the best of his tech was in a much safer location.

Her heels thudded into the hard floor, charcoal carpet tiles muffling the spiked ends, as she glided between desks and the giant wall of glass separating Old Syd's robbery detectives from the light and thunder of the city itself.

The sun might have left the sky eight hours ago, and the recent winter-snap might have frozen the smog layer to the streets forty levels below, but the buildings and busy skylanes made up for it. Hovers zipped past the big plate windows, the smart glass struggling to block the glare, a giant reflection of the lights pulsing in the police officers' eyes.

A dozen of them, all rooted to their desks, the floor, or in the case of the beard in the interrogation room, both.

The beard... Malone had been the name on the holographic shield above his watch when he'd "invited" her down to the precinct for a chat. Only one of Detective Sergeant Malone's eyes had pulsed, while the other... Clear and green as newly mown grass, glazed with pain instead of the sheen of an ocular implant.

That had been a nasty little surprise. Trust her to find the one luddite in the precinct, although the restraints on the interrogation chair should hold a whacked-out jarhead.

'Dorothy, time to the security reboot?'

// Seventeen minutes.

Enough time. More than enough time. Unless Malone shucked his restraints. Just her luck to catch the attention of the luddite in Old Syd's robbery division. Her luck had been like that recently. Good, then enough to curdle her insides.

Her heels echoed in the silence.

◊

Malone pushed himself off the floor through sheer, teeth-baring grit. The restraints capturing his wrists had helped him resist the urge to rip his eyeball out, right up until they popped, freeing him. By that time he was gripping the arms so tight he'd lost the feeling in his fingers, was sure he'd cracked a tooth and that tendons in his neck had torn the flesh, only REX's quiet, *// S– Serrrgeant* had broken him from it.

And now… every muscle in his body shook, from his fingers to his arms, his chest, his toes. The damn disco in his right eye turned the interrogation room in a kind of hell, closing it helped about as much as a snowball in that fine place.

Lights still strobed and pulsed inside his lid, liquifying his brain, but at least the interrogation room didn't dip and wave, and the open door didn't pulsate with his heart.

Didn't stop him staggering, didn't do jack shit for the motherfucking headache. But he was upright, and even if he shuffled—bent and stiff as an old man—he was moving. Which was more than he could say for his fellows out in the bullpen.

Rayes was slumped over her desk, her partner twitching on the dark-grey carpet. And there, half-propped against the floor-to-ceiling windows overlooking the skylane, was the lieutenant, a grey cast to her otherwise brown skin.

He grunted as he stumbled to Rayes' desk, thigh making friends with the corner. The detective was staring straight ahead and there was a disco going on in her eyes. He pushed her aside, gentle, or as gentle as he could when he wasn't quite sure where his hands were, or which muscles made his fingers work, but he managed it. Reached for the phone...

The sliver of glass and plastic lit up at skin contact, was cool against his ear. And silent.

He pulled it away, studied it with his one good eye. Tried to decide if the static running through the interface was the light-show or a System fritz. Tapped out a command override with a thick, tatted finger, just in case and held it to his ear again.

Nothing.

He held it there a second longer. Tapped the mouthpiece.

Only the banshee answered.

'Fuck.' He dropped the handset, almost sure it fell on the desk, not quite sure if it fell on Rayes on the desk. But there were other things to worry about.

Like the dame.

Where was the dame?

There it was.

She crouched in front of the case, her dress reflecting in the smart glass, shoes sparking light around the vault like a disco. Beyond her reflection, not Old Man Arend's diamonds—the fake ones, all light without substance—but the real thing. Carbon squashed beyond imagining, spit out into the world on the liquid breath of Earth herself.

She smiled.

Not what she was after, but pretty… and expected.

She tapped the dragon wound around her ankle. 'Time to go to work, Dorothy.'

// If you say so, Lorelei.

'Oh, I do, I very, very much do.'

One by one, the glittering stones that made up the twin dragons fell from her shoes, little *tink tink tinks* echoing on the cold concrete. She didn't watch them, Dorothy had it covered and there were other things to consume her attention. Like the databanks buried under the floor.

She got up, stepping out of the stilettos—little more than strappy platforms now, impossible to walk in without the dragons to hold them to her feet—and padded precisely one-point-zero-one metres into the middle of the grey and silver vault. There was nothing there, not even a mark in the pale-grey concrete, but then who drew an "X" over the valuables?

Besides, Dorothy was good.

She stood there for a few moments—twenty-eight seconds according to the timer on her interface—enough time for the nano-liner attached to her soles to scan the ground, before giving the concrete a quick, hard stomp with her heel. No hollow echo, not even a rattle came back, just the full fleshy sound of skin on aggregate.

'Dorothy? Confirm.'

// Analysing data... Confirmed, Lorelei.

A diagram appeared on the floor around her feet, one just for her. A rectangle one metre wide by sixty-eight centimetres long and ten deep, with an interface transcribed on it in eye-searing blue.

She allowed herself a smile and knelt, gold sequins splitting over her knee. She twisted the big square stone on her ring finger before pressing it and her palm to the middle of the interface on her HUD.

'Dorothy, run the program.'

// Yes, Lorelei.

A wall of code flew past her eye, and there was a tingle under her skin, lifting the hairs along her nape and down her left arm, all the way to the diamond ring pressed to the floor.

For a moment, nothing happened, and then the brilliant blue-white outline on the HUD became reality, light lifting out of the dove-grey concrete to surround her hand. Another buzz and—

'Authorisation required,' appeared simultaneously on the HUD and the floor, along with the outline of a hand.

Another ring, this one a white-gold band with a delicate inlay of platinum, the better to conduct the nanites embedded in the metal. And this time, it wasn't her arm or nape that fizzed, but her palm. Hot and furious, not just over her skin but under it, as the smart skin crawled, masking the patterns in her skin, giving her the detective's palm print, while the nanites in her blood adjusted the rush to her palm, altered her heart rate to match the detective's.

Under her, the interface winked green.

A heavy *clunk* felt as much as heard shivered through her soles.

She stood and stepped back.

The rectangle of floor glowed a moment then popped down and sideways, leaving a rectangular pit in the middle of the vault.

Lorelei peered over the edge

Fairy lights, in twinkling red and green and blue, festooned the computer stored below.

She smiled and unhooked the diamond waterfall from her ear, the stones another buzz against her palm.

'Dorothy,' she said. 'Brace yourself.'

◊

'Authorisation required.'

Lorelei stared at the interface, all expression wiped from her face, eyes flecks of jade.

'Dorothy, time,' she said.

// Four minutes, eighteen seconds Lorelei.

She didn't swear, didn't let a frown mar her brow or pull the corners of lips. Frowning put lines at the corners of her eyes and ruined the smooth dip between her perfectly sculpted brows. And glaring... crow's feet and stress, an additional dose of cortisol shot into her bloodstream, another load on her heart. Her heart didn't need another load, didn't need anything except the glittering hoard beyond the Robbery and Serious Crime Squad's reinforced titanium floor.

And so, for a whole thirty luxurious seconds, she did nothing except focus on those two words as if she could vanish them with will alone.

The second encryption layer hadn't been in the schematics, but she'd still prepared for it, or something like it. Always make allowances for arseholes, arsenals, and the little gleam in Old Man Arend's eye, and so she'd had a backup plan ready – all those detectives hostage to their ocular implants, retinal scans just a query away. The third layer though…

Her luck had turned again.

She'd have to leave Arend a special little gift once this was over.

'Authorisation required.'

'Dorothy,' she said. 'Status.'

In the pit, the glittering swirl of nano-diamonds that was the AI's second skin, paused.

// A live biological match is required for this lock, Lorelei.

'Biological?'

// A bodily fluid would be ideal.

She glanced over her shoulder to the bullpen of bodily fluids – a full forty-nine-second sprint down the security corridor and through the coded lock. Dorothy focused again on the vault, still firmly closed over its prize.

In the corner of her left eye, the counter ticked past three minutes.

She didn't have time for this.

If she could just—

The cold point of a muzzle against her nape.

Her luck, it seemed, could get worse.

'Don't move,' a low, rough voice ground out.

But then again…

She knew that voice.

Lorelei smiled even as she raised her hands to her shoulders, palms out, fingers splayed as that muzzle shifted, pushing aside her hair as weapon and man circled to stand in front of her. The blocky pistol looked just right in the detective's tatted hands.

She widened her smile, let her head tilt so she wasn't staring down the barrel of the carbon-black pistol, and watched his one open eye follow the movement of her hair. 'Detective,' she said. 'How's the—?'

A high pitched whine interrupted her, and a blue light travelled down the pistol barrel to pool in the little divot below the sight.

'Not a muscle,' he said.

'Now.' She leaned back, watched the detective's good eye slide south as the split in her gown rode up over her thigh. 'That would be a shame,' she said.

◇

The dame's legs really were something to die for, but he wasn't dying today, not even for those long, lean works for art.

Malone steadied his aim, pistol in two hands, one eye closed against the psychedelic kaleidoscope going off behind the lid.

His skull was three sizes too small for his grey matter, but at least he was standing. Small mercies.

'Hands behind your head,' he said.

'Now, Detective—'

He stepped forward, pressed the muzzle between the dame's sculpted brows. 'Your head.'

Those hands came up, slow, sure, the diamond ring on her index finger sending a spear right through his eyeball.

She lunged, the pistol flew out of his hands, and one of the long, long legs sent him tumbling to the floor after it. For a second, a single triumphant second, he had the upper hand and then—

◇

With a twist and a flip, it was no longer her on the bottom but Malone, the detective's chest pressed to the cold titanium floor, her knee pressed into his back, her arm around his throat and his face… His face hovering precisely twenty-eight centimetres over the flashing black interface in the floor and with a little help from her ring, his blood drop, drop, dropping.

'Authorisation accepted.'

Perfect—

Malone was part eel, that was the only explanation she had as he slipped through her hold, skin and shirt and old jeans too slippery to be real. One moment she was staring past his whiskey buzz cut to the vault parting over a glittering array of nano-diamonds, and the next… Oh, if only she'd met the detective in a different guise.

Maybe next time.

They twisted on the floor, Malone on top, superior weight pinning her… Until she hooked a leg around his neck and then the detective was on the bottom, one meaty hand wrapped around her thigh, trying to stop her squeezing the air out of him, the other going for her neck – damn his long arms.

Back and forth they went, neither getting the upper hand until he threw her sideways.

She rolled across the concrete, the sharp vault edge bitting her back, hand finding a warm, familiar block as Malone staggered to his feet. Came at her.

Her fingers curled around the pistol, finding the little groove for the trigger as she brought it up.

The detective stopped cold.

The pistol whined, light shining blue from the divot under the sight all the way down the barrel.

She gave it a beat, a single thump of her pulse, enough for the detective's hard green gaze to skip past the muzzle to lock with her own, and smiled.

'Thanks for the diamonds,' she said and shot.

A Country Event

INTRODUCTION

In my hometown we have an annual short story competition. Although I always resolve to do so, I never manage to submit anything; I'm always in the midst of writing something else or what I do write for the competition *becomes* something else. Like this story.

Originally, *A Country Event* (the theme for last year's competition) was meant to be about the shenanigans at a country wedding, and it still is, just… with a supernatural bent. A *very* supernatural bent, so supernatural in fact that I went "what the hell" and decided it belonged with my other rural fantasy stories, *Corpses & Demon Horses* and *Little Black Book*.

And that, dear reader, is how a series is born; it creeps up on you like a big ol' bay trotting up a dirt track, or an editor feeding the plot bunnies.

A COUNTRY EVENT

The sun was setting behind the old shearing shed up on the hill. The red and orange blazing behind the rusty corrugated walls and roof, making long shadows out of the squat concrete water tank at its side.

The warm spring breeze wound through the bars of the sheep yards beside the shed, picking up the smell of lanolin and sheep shit along with the leaves as it blew through the pines lining the long drive.

She wrinkled her nose as she got out of the car, Western boots sinking to the ankle in pine needles and sour-sobs. The stench of concentrated sheep shit had never sat well with her, even diluted by distance and the earthy scent of the old pines; there was something about the way it sat on the back of her tongue that curdled her tastebuds.

Niyha picked up her long black skirt and tromped through the grass, short Cuban heels sliding a little in the damp. The old dirt drive was firm enough when she reached it, there was even fresh gravel in the potholes. If she came out of this with just a muddy skirt hem, soggy socks and a job done, she'd count herself lucky.

Not that luck had been with her of late.

She started up the half-kilometre of drive toward the house.

Cars packed the spaces under the spreading branches all the way from the gates where'd she'd parked, to the house yard.

Her old black ute didn't even look of place amongst the pimped out utes and early-model sedans. It was freshly washed for the occasion, all the way from the rearview mirror with its cracked glass, to the tray. She'd even gone so far as to wash the floor mats, nearly killed her vacuum with the mud and little stones caught in the footwell, and strained her back hauling the lockboxes off and then back on the tray. The red one, especially. It'd needed a little extra care, as it always did lest she trigger the spells sunk in its battered metal sides.

Either Debbie's rich city friends had got here early, or (more likely) she'd persuaded Dad to reserve spots for them closer to the house. The further she walked up the winding drive, the more the utes and four wheel drives gave way to SUVs and sleek sedans, with the odd space left for the other vehicles, like the Pattersons' buggy and the Jones's brooms. The latter poking out of what looked like hastily-made brackets, sleek bulbous ends looking more like fat tulips than lean moon-fuelled engines.

There were enough brooms there to clean the shearing shed for the next century.

The Jones's had brought the whole clan it seemed.

She straightened her back and made sure the protective amulets on her corset were aligned.

Her estimation of her luck this night went down another notch.

She paused a moment, half-turned back to her ute. Nibbled her lip.

Maybe she should get the extra hex wards out of the red trunk? Shook her head.

No, Old Woman Jones didn't do weddings. Although there was one Niyha was half-way certain the crone would make an exception for.

She shuddered.

Starting forward again, she lifted her skirts higher as she side-stepped a puddle Dad's drive-repair had missed. Although, it was more likely all the vehicles to and fro—first setting up for the wedding than the guests—had eroded the surface. It wouldn't have taken much, not with the rain through the week.

It was a long walk to the house, a good ten minutes from where she'd parked down near the gate. If she'd caved to her sister's wheedling and stayed the night before, she'd have avoided it, but then she'd have to put up with Debbie's Bridezilla impersonation.

She'd rather face Old Woman Jones.

At least she'd gone with the cowboy boots instead of the spiky heels, even if she'd rather the rest of the outfit stayed locked in the back of the closet. But there were some things that called for armour, and Bridezilla Debbie was one of them.

The corset made breathing a challenge and black did nothing for her pale skin except make her look like a corpse, while the brocaded silk skirts—not just one, but three, counting the underskirt and petticoat—embroidered with snakes and archaic signs, made running a hazard.

Not that there'd be running tonight, she thought, even as she twisted her fingers in a sign against bad luck.

No running, not even a jog. Hell, not even a dance if she could get away with it. She'd just slip in the back, drop off the gift, kiss her mum on the cheek, straighten her dad's tie and make sure Debbie latched eyes on her before high-tailing it back down the drive.

All before the moon rose above the old hay shed.

She crossed her fingers.

An hour, max, and she'd be dust and headlights bumping down the corrugated road to her little piece of heaven.

The house was just ahead, music and happy voices filtering through the straight old pines as the drive took a turn. With the setting sun filtering through the rough trunks and the straight branches reaching overhead, the drive was magical, even with the parking lot of vehicles and brooms. She let herself imagine she was walking to a different wedding, one without the fancy band, expensive shoes, and plastic chairs covered in white silk and wrapped in pink organza bows.

It didn't take much. The memories swarmed from the back of her mind, bringing with them the gentle warmth of another spring day, the smell of hay and the bite of beer. There was even the steady *clop clop* of a horse coming up behind, the jangle of a bit and the soft slap of reins against leather. In fact, if she turned—

—she'd stare down a familiar white-faced bay, black forelock flopping between his dark red ears, camouflaging his eyes. She knew those eyes, one a ghostly blue the other deep chocolate, knew he hated her patting sunscreen on his velvety pink muzzle, how he'd wriggle his lip and toss his head. But never bite. Buddy was too much a gentlemen to ever do something so crude—

Knew what she'd see too, if she lifted her gaze a little higher, to between the short, curved ears.

Fuck. Ben.

The real Ben and not the one in her memory.

She spun on her heel.

Keep walking, Niyha. Keep walking.

Buddy's half-ton shadow crept up beside her, head then neck then chest, fancy hand-tooled breastplate attached to a saddle… then a leg.

A leg in new, dark-blue jeans, the hems brushing a worn leather boot with a pointed toe and Cuban heel. Freshly scrubbed, just like her ute, but with a new coat of pale dirt dusting the sides, same as her hems. If she looked down.

Fucked if she was looking down.

She tossed her hair back, the mane—black and glossy, just like Buddy's—the twisty ends loose, brushing the small of her back. She'd be paying for that decision come evening, or fuck, come morning if she didn't escape Debbie's evil Bridezilla claws; those same curly ends would be tangled to buggery and she'd be rethinking her life choices along with the combing. But it was necessary; in the way that a Pap smear was necessary; if not for her pleasure then at least her good health.

For however long that lasted.

Probably not long, if the jean-clad leg and the shadow were anything to go by. Who knows, maybe she'd get even *luckier* and Old Woman Jones had received her parcel early. The little gift that just kept giving.

Fuck, she shouldn't have got out of bed.

Buddy flicked his ear back and shook his head, disagreeing with whatever Ben had silently asked.

Ben slapped the reins against the horse's side.

Another head-shake, and this time a gust of air against her back as he flicked his tail.

Ben clicked his tongue.

Buddy heaved a sigh, and just as Niyha started to wonder what Ben was asking, the big red horse picked himself up and launched into a trot.

She stopped dead. That... hadn't been what she expected, she thought, as man and horse trotted up the drive, big steel-shod hooves kicking up dust to play in the sunlight. Where was the 'hello', the slow drawl and lazy conversation that always got her back up, the dig about the hair, the skirts, the—?

Buddy skidded to a stop two metres ahead, sunk on his hindquarters and spun like a ballerina. Even before he finished twisting, Ben was leaning forward, weight over Buddy's neck, legs kicking back...

Oh shit. She started walking again, fast as her skirts and cowboy boots would take her.

...Ben's boots hitting the drive, kicking up their own little cloud of dust to play in the sun, arse looking fine in those dark-blue jeans, back long and lean in the red shirt, pleats nice and crisp up the back. Freshly ironed. And not by her, thank Goddess.

Fuck, fuck, fuck. And her boots couldn't take her fast enough, the skirts—thin as they were, despite the embroidery—too voluminous for true speed, not without running.

She wouldn't run, she *wouldn't.*

Quick and graceful as his fucking horse, unhindered by the

wide-brimmed felted Akubra shoved low on his chestnut head, Ben turned, caught her bare arm just as she drew even with Buddy's rump.

The electric *snap* that travelled from her to him lit up the twilight and left ozone on the air. They yelped and Buddy skittered sideways.

She pulled away, put a good couple of steps between them and glared, wishing now she'd grabbed Gran's old shawl off the passenger seat, just so her skin wouldn't fuzz with yet more memories.

Ben glared back at her, dark-chestnut brows pulled low over eyes the colour of spring pastures and a nose crooked from one-too-many arguments with livestock… and that one with her.

'You gotta talk to me sometime, Niyha,' he said, that sinfully deep voice reaching across the dirt to run fingers up her spine.

Fuck him.

'I don't gotta do shit, Ben.' And wouldn't it be grand if her own tones were as dulcet as the arsehole's staring her down. Genetics might have given her luscious black locks and just enough cleavage to fill out her corset, but her voice was better suited to yelling curses across the sheep pen.

She spun on her heel and—

Buddy was there, quicker than an animal with more muscles in his chest than a bodybuilder on steroids had any right to be. The horse blocked her way with his rump, backing up when she tried to go around, all the way to the fancy black Mercedes parked beside a beat up Prado. (Someone had gotten through Debbie's shield of rich.)

It was Buddy's turn to receive a glare.

'Just whose side are you on, Buddy?'

The quarter horse flicked a black-tipped ear and shook his head but didn't say a word.

She went to go around the other way... but Ben was there. Ben was always fucking *there*.

She sidestepped.

Ben stepped with her.

Sidestepped the other way.

Again, Ben was there.

She hiked up her skirts, bent at the waist to duck under Buddy's belly and—

Ben was there on the horse's other side when she popped up.

How had the bastard done that?

A hiss escaped Niyha's lips, annoyance and the first hints of magic staining the air purple.

'Get outta my way, Ben.' And that was a growl, all gravelly and just the right kinda mean for her sheep-pen voice.

He shook his head, shoved his thumbs in his jean pockets and set his feet, boots digging into the dirt drive. 'Ain't going to do it.'

She was in his space, black, amulet-studded corset to crisp red shirt, snake-embroidered silk pressed up again bone-buttoned cotton. Even with the quarter-inch heels, the top of her head barely came to his nose. Lifting up on her toes brought her teeth even with his chin.

She flashed them. 'You will move,' and the words came out low, another puff of purple floating in the hands-breadth between their faces.

An answering emerald spark lit his gaze. 'Make me.'

Niyha hissed, and on her corset a black-embroidered snake, its belly blood-red, unwound from under her breast, while an unfelt wind lifted the ends of her hair.

At her back, Buddy *whuffed*.

The emerald in Ben's eyes shone a little brighter, an answering light cracking around his knuckles. A different wind played with the dark-chestnut hair curled against his nape.

She really hated those curls, they always distracted her at the worst possible—

Ben's dimples only came out when he smirked. Like now.

Another hiss, and the other snake under her other breast lifted its head, the wind now picking up her hems and dragging hair across her face.

Debbie'd kill her if she made a scene at the wedding, but the house was still around the bend, and there was no one coming up the drive. Who was going to venture out from the marquees with their silk-covered tables laden with fancy champagne and expensive food the size of her thumb? No one, that's who, and if they did, so what? Ben was asking for it.

Ben'd been asking for it for months now, ever since his cousin, Graven Jones, got in her face and said the kind of words no warlock ever said to a witch. Not even the nice ones.

And no one called her nice. Not on full moon, not on a dark moon, nor any of the nights in between. Not even on a dare.

In Druford, smart people knew better than the fuck with a Durant witch, and the idiots who didn't, rarely survived long. Darwinism, Durant-style.

She stared at Ben.

Ben stared back.

If only he wasn't a fucking *Jones*.

But then, if wishes were unicorns she'd have a stud full of 'em by now.

The embroidered snakes twisted around her breasts and slithered over her collarbones, while her lips, painted blush pink for the occasion—not her usual purple, at Debbie's request—moved without sound.

The light in Ben's eyes spilled through his iris as her hair whipped around and the snakes reached her hands. Magic turned the sunlight purple and green, cracked and seethed.

Just as the power building in Niyha's chest reached her fingertips, begging to spill into the world; just as Ben shifted, closing the last little bit of air between them, green snapping over his hands, daring her—

The head-shattering *crack* split them apart.

One moment they were chest-to-chest, magic seething, the next

Niyha was hanging off Buddy's saddle, both hands wrapped around the horn, glad the horse wasn't the kind to spook. And Ben… Ben was on his arse in the pine needles and dewy grass, that fucking hat *still* on his head, a little magic still sparking his eyes but none cracking across his knuckles.

A scorch mark and a new pothole stood when she and Ben had just a moment before.

A Crone stood on its other side, her back to the mansion. A faint green shimmer gilded her slim, straight shoulders making it easy to pick out the strands of salted grey in the chestnut hair piled atop her head. She'd obviously just come from the reception.

So much for everyone being busy with the food.

And so much for Old Woman Jones' aversion to weddings.

And fuck it, if that wasn't a globe from a certain parcel in the old woman's hands.

It could be any globe, of course; a snow globe, a paperweight, a fist-sized marble made of green-threaded quartz, but the way Niyha's luck was going…

A frown creased the Crone's unnaturally smooth forehead, creased deep enough to bury a body.

Behind her, Buddy—the quarter horse who hadn't flapped when lightning hit the ground not a metre from him—skittered sideways, dragging Niyha with him.

Hastily, she let go of the saddle horn before she lost her footing.

Buddy bolted.

Smart horse.

'Mrs Jones—' she started.

A slim, bony hand stopped her.

'Out of the dirt, boy.' Ben'd got his voice from his grandmother's side of the family. Even with the damning globe in her hand and anger rumbling on her words, Old Woman Jones could charm a snake out of its skin.

Or a Durant out of hers.

Whatever worked.

The Jones' weren't fussy like that.

Niyha backed up a step. 'It's a wedding, Mrs Jones.'

Old Woman Jones' eyes were emerald, dark and deep, not the bright yellow-green of her grandson, and where his had *snapped*, hers heaved.

'Yes, it is,' said the Crone, and somehow, Niyah knew the old woman wasn't talking about Debbie's.

Niyha swallowed and wished she'd gone back for the extra hex wards.

So much power in such a frail frame, it was almost enough to make a Durant witch jealous. Almost, but not quite. The benefits to being a Durant were more than just idiot-stomping.

Out the corner of her eye, she clocked Ben, back on his feet and hands out to his sides. 'Gran,' he began, whiskey-smooth voice reaching across the dirt, all calm and reason.

But the old woman shut him down; an eyebrow twitch, and while Ben's mouth moved, no sound came out.

The old woman only had eyes for her.

And Nihya... Niyha wasn't sure whether to meet them or watch the globe in the bony hands. The globe she'd sent just the other day, by accident, because that was just her luck.

And the moon not even risen yet.

Fuck.

'Mrs Jones,' she began again, taking a step forward as she did, hoping against hope it didn't look as nervous and shaky as it felt. 'I really didn't—'

Old Woman Jones held the oversized quartz marble at chest height, hoisting it on the tips of her fingers like some kind of trophy. 'You know what this is.' It wasn't a question.

Niyha swallowed again. She nodded. 'Yes.'

She'd sent it, after all.

'And so you know what it means when a witch opens up a nice little parcel, expecting her favourite tea, only to find something like this inside.' And did the driveway dirt shudder under the

Crone's pointed black shoes, or was that Fate running a cold, clammy hand down her spine?

Another nod, another swallow, all the spit gone from her mouth. 'I do,' she said. And that was a benefit of a voice like a Durant, didn't matter if it cracked, she always sounded like her vocal cords'd been dragged over rocks.

Old Woman Jones returned the nod, the *snapping* emeralds keeping hold of Niyha's, unblinking pools of power.

So much power.

The snakes on her corset slithered to her back.

'Good.' Old Woman Jones stopped, just three short strides between them now. She held out the globe, and like the obedient little stone it was, it lifted off the old woman's fingers and hovered between them, the mossy green and white lit up from within. 'Then you'll be able to explain to your sister why you messed up her little shindig.'

Well, shit.

∗

Debbie was not happy, not that any of the fancy guests could tell, not even Dad or her new husband. But Niyha knew, and Mum standing on Debbie's other side, up on the little dais with the main table. The one for the family and bridal party, just a little step above the rest of the marquee, not so much the guests would notice. All the better for them to survey the bride in her white, lace glory, and for the bride to survey them. Her little fiefdom of Gucci and Prada, guarded by the John Deeres and the old Masey bulldozer not even Mum's grumbling could get Dad to displace.

Her younger sister didn't do anything so crass as glower, that would give her lines, but she held her chin higher and she never could help the ever so slight furrow over her nose. But it was the aura more than anything that gave her away. All the discipline Debbie put into controlling her face and posture came straight off the control over the things regular folk didn't see. Like the purple-red flames snapping around her shoulders, their ghostly shadow clinging to her hair – the same black locks as Niyha's, except swept up into a confection of curls atop her head.

Niyha shifted her feet, yellow gravel crunching under her western boots, black skirts muffling the sound, her own hair curling around her elbows.

Night and day they were, or Debbie tried hard to make them appear.

Sometimes, Niyha wondered why she bothered.

Sometimes, but not now. Now she just wanted to snatch the oversized green quartz marble from Old Woman Jones' hand and stomp out of the marquee. Rid her nose of the baskets of white roses and baby's breath on their Corinthian pedestals and her ears of the whispers shooting from one round table to another.

A little fire, a lotta smoke and maybe—just maybe—a little help from the returned Buddy, and she'd be halfway down the drive before the Crone—and Debbie—finished sorting out the hoo-ha. She cast a glance at Ben, standing a step behind and to her left, in just the right spot to obscure his hands and face from her sight, but not enough to remain out of it.

If she were real lucky, the distraction would work as well on Ben as the rest.

Dappled green light fell on her face as Old Woman Jones lifted the quartz globe high, her power pulsing through it.

But then again, her luck was kinda shit today.

Fuck.

She should've stayed in bed.

'I have a reckoning.' The whispers died as Old Woman Jones' voice rang through the tent.

Niyha fingered one of the hex wards on her corset, trying—and failing—not to look at the cluster of chestnut heads and green eyes to her right. She was half surprised the Jones clan didn't back up the old woman's words with an angelic hum, just for effect.

The norms in the crowd hushed and the witches stopped

whispering. The collective silence shot up to the fairy-light-strung canvas roof and hovered there a moment, before a loud equine snort brought it crashing down.

At least Buddy wasn't worried.

Under her sleeves, Niyha crossed her fingers and prayed the quarter horse didn't wander off. She was still hoping for that stroke of good luck, that turning tide in her very shitty week—

Up on the bridal table, an old tomcat stalked in front of the plates and wine glasses, the ghostly black apparition passing through the white and gold flower arrangements with the same casual arrogance he'd had in life. He stared at her as he did, eyes that'd been green in life a deep purple-violet in death.

Well, shit.

So much for the good luck.

She could practically *feel* the old feline fucker smiling.

'A reckoning,' Old Woman Jones said again – and screw her sideways, if the Jones clan didn't *actually* hum this time. 'Sent by a Durant.'

And no, she'd been wrong before, Buddy's unconcerned snort hadn't brought the weight of all those indrawn breaths crashing down, that had just been the preview, the taster before the old woman delivered her coup de grace.

An anvil— No, a *hundred* anvils landed on Niyha's shoulders, a silent crushing weight turning her knees to water, making her thighs tremble and back sag. She staggered, found the back of a silk-shrouded plastic chair and heard the *crack* as her weight fell on it, the exclamation as it teetered back, toupee'd occupant and all.

Was it the power in Old Woman Jones' words, the hum from the clan, or was it the globe itself, the spells worked into the polished stone? Or worse yet, was it Debbie, all that anger finally swamping her face even as it snaked through her aura – purple serpents snapping their tails and spitting venom?

The snakes embroidered on Niyha's own corset stirred with the power in her middle, the wind picking up her curls and playing with her skirts. They hissed and slid around her breasts, over her shoulders, while the wind stiffened her knees, let her push against the weight trying to hold her down.

A hand on her arm—Ben's familiar, warm, horsey scent—helped her stand straight and let go of the chair.

Fuck, if only the postie had been a day later.

Just twelve hours was all it would have taken, long enough for the new moon to pass and weigh the balance of magic in favour of the Durants.

But now... All those Joneses green eyes slid from their matriarch to little ol' her, in her black corset and loose curls, as far removed from Debbie in all her virgin white glory as it was possible to get and still share a face.

Or most of a face. Debbie'd missed out on the thick lashes and cupid bow mouth, much to her younger sister's disgust.

Of course, Debbie got all the good luck in exchange. Except for now, with her older-by-eleven-minutes-and-don't-you-forget-it sister raining shit all over her wedding.

Niyha lifted her chin and put a little extra steel in her spine.

Old Woman Jones turned and her eyes were emerald flames.

Niyha's step back was instinct—fire is hot, don't touch it—but Ben's solid presence at her spine had her coming up short.

On the bridal table, the old tomcat leapt, the ghost stalking from one round guest table to another, winding his way closer.

Fucker had always liked a scene.

Best day of her damn life when Fox had got him.

Bastard.

No time for that though, the rest of the Jones clan was standing now, weaving though the marquee in the tomcat's wake—did they see him?—and the old woman was holding the globe out, the green quartz still resting the tips of her bony fingers, her shawl-draped arms seeming to stretch and stretch and stretch like one of those carnival mirrors.

And Niyha with Ben at her back and nowhere to go. And even if she got out of there, even if the moon had passed out the other side of full, there was still Debbie, still the globe, still Graven Jones and his stupid face. The face she'd taught a lesson to, Durant style.

Her eyes slid past Old Woman Jones, meeting Debbie's furious purple ones over the tops of the green-eyed clan fanning out in a semi-circle around her.

Okay, so maybe not the Druford Durant style, all nicey nice with the rich folk, pillars of the community.

Maybe catching Graven Jones as he came out of his favourite drinking hole at the darkest height of the month and introducing him to the inside of the globe was a little too old-school Durant. But at least it wasn't a book, and at least she planned on giving him back.

A month in quartz wouldn't have hurt him.

Much.

The quartz hovered under her nose.

Old Woman Jones looked at her over the top.

Niyha met her gaze for gaze, magic for magic.

The hush descended again. Only the Jones clan's *hum* kept it from snapping shut all around.

The old woman raised a single chestnut brow. *Well?* it said.

'I'm still not marrying him,' Niyha responded. 'Not even as a paperweight.'

THE POLAR BEAR

INTRODUCTION

My working title for this story was 'Polar Bear in a Snowstorm'. It's an art joke from my university days, where we'd hold up a piece of blank paper and proudly proclaim that we'd drawn a picture of a polar bear in a snowstorm.

It's funny the first time and every other time… I don't know, the idea of the blank page as a snowstorm likes to sit with me and pops up whenever I start a new story. We could get terribly philosophical and imagine that the story is a snowstorm out of which the author pulls and shapes words into a tangible picture but… That way lies another story and my books-to-write list is very, *very* long.

In any case, the main character in this tale *is* a polar bear and he is, in fact, travelling through a snowstorm with a very precious, kinda scary cargo on his back.

THE POLAR BEAR

The bear stalked.

Heavy, white fur blended with the storm, paws silent as he trudged through banks up to his belly. He didn't feel the cold, the icicles hanging from his chest, the snow pushing through his thick, padded toes. Took no notice of the ice nor the rocks hidden under the drifts, barely acknowledged the trees rising tall and silent all around, their presence felt more than seen – as invisible as the bear in their layers of frost. And of the weight on his back... An insignificant thing. Tiny. Barely worth mentioning. Yet he carried it with the gravitas of fresh spilled blood, of souls scattered across the divide. He slowed his strides and added caution to his paws.

The sun had yet to fall, and yet all that could be seen was white. Perfect, endless white darkened here by a tree, there by an embankment. Although not the bear's shadow or the shadow of the one on his back. If one looked close though, they might have seen his eyes, black as the stillest night without cloud or moon, just the stars hanging high up, cold and pitiless. And if one were to see his eyes... The bear hummed to himself, a rumble ripped away by the wind. If a thing came close enough to see his eyes, there would be a new colour on his muzzle, a new warmth in his belly.

The wind was a ferocious howl fit to shred even mage-born muffles and deafen the ear. All ears but the bear's—those were tucked deep in the thick coat around his neck—and the woman's atop his back.

The storm obscured her as much as the bear, but it was the heavy, fur-lined cloak, the thick woollen robes and fleece-lined boots that made her invisible. In that moment, if the storm had ceased and snow had fallen where it blew, she and her steed would still have faded into the nothing of that forest.

White on ivory on palest blue and pearliest white. That's what the eye would have seen, a mound atop a furry, night-eyed mound amongst the snow.

But the wind didn't die, and there wasn't another soul out on that frozen mountain even if it had. Just the bear, his burden, and the cave they left far behind.

The storm lessened. Died a little as they came out of the foothills of that mountain. The forest was a smudge on the horizon, the shadows under its heavy branches a dove grey against the cold pearl, coating the mountain as surely as the snow covered them. There were farms in the foothills, hidden under snowdrifts, houses under mounds of the same. Only the smoke twisting in the still air gave hint to life within.

The bear ignored the roads, just as he ignored fences. Even if he could have seen them, he would have walked over. He knew where he was going and such things as pathways and boundaries meant little to him. There were none such where he came from, only ice that broke from its moorings, snow that blew from one place to another, and a freezing ocean that never stilled.

He did not think the one atop his back gave such human concerns much mind either. Did not think one such as her gave much mind to anything, unless, of course, it was blood.

Hot, spurting, steaming as it hit the air, coating the cave walls.

He hummed.

A thing to ponder, and ponder he had on the long stalk down

the mountain.

Ponder what came next, ponder the little village at the bottom, a place he'd never been but had seen in the mage-born's tales. A strange place, with caves made of trees and humans wrapped in fur. Wolf fur, grey and black and dark-mottled white. Bear fur, brown and black, but not white. Not polar fur, but the stupid, unenlightened brethren of the mountains.

And now, as they came out of the foothills and woodsmoke twisted in the wind, bringing with it the smells of sheep and cow and goat laid over flames as the humans liked it, he didn't have to ponder anymore. He saw. He scented.

He understood what had prompted his burden to push her way through snow up to her waist. What had driven her out of the rift in the stars dressed only her thin human skin, what had made her brave the ice and wind and snow. Why she had smelled of blood and rage, why she had painted the cave at the top of the mountain. More, he understood why he was here, in the village, now, with this burden.

A terrible burden.

A joyful one.

He would remember it for the rest of his years.

His burden directed him to a building bigger than others, double the height with three smoke-spewing holes in the roof instead of one. It was big enough that the snow had yet to pile to the windows at the top, letting yellow light spill into the growing dark.

Sounds spilled with it, pushing through the walls and piled snow. Human sounds. Voices raised with laughter and song, and more of those smells – heated sheep and cow, mixed with something strange and sharp. He had no name for it, but he remembered it from the cave, how it mixed with blood, strong and heady.

It would mix here too, he thought. Stronger. Without the cold and wind to wipe it away.

He would have walked right to the building's opening—'door', the mage-born had called it—pawed open the wood and squeezed himself and his burden inside, but she whispered for him to stop.

A strange sound, his burden's voice. A soft melody as if with many voices, slipping and sliding through his ears. He was not sure if it was his ears that heard it, or if she made herself understood in some other way – like the wind, or the fish slipping under the ice-flows. Shadows felt in his paws and the hairs along his back.

Whatever it was, she commanded and he stopped outside the building's boundary, more walls piled with snow, with a large square opening in their centre. Beyond the open space, the drifts lessened, enough to see the frozen ground—brown-black and pebbled with pale yellow—and straw-mixed shit was piled in one corner, chopped wood in another, but it was the door that held his attention.

That and his burden slipping her feet out of the fleece-lined stirrups, her leg over his neck. She slid to the ground, graceful, soft, not even a muffled *thud* when her feet met the ground. Her cloak with its deep hood—the fleece lining stiff with ice—made her larger than she was. That, and the robes under it. He recalled her in the cave, how slight, how small, how the blood stood out against her white, white skin.

He looked again to the door, and then to his burden. Studied the size of her against the sounds he could tell from within— thunks and thuds and clangs, hoarse shouts and higher squeals, pigs stuck in a pen—and he did not like it.

She glided past him.

He kept a pace behind, all the way to the door, to the light and the meat and the stench.

She turned, placed a slim, pale hand on his forehead, between his eyes—the skin soft and smooth, with a dry musty scent—and said, 'No.'

No.

And so he stopped and sat and waited while she opened the door and disappeared within.

He sat and waited for long, long moments, straining his ears for the *shush* of her cloak, the near-silent pad of her feet, prising them out from under the other sounds as he prised her scent from the air. It was difficult at first, stretched his senses to their limits, and then it wasn't.

The laughter and shouts, the squeals and thumps faded. Stopped.

Turned to screams.

The screams lasted moments. Moments in which a human—not his burden—yanked open the door, a tall male with fur crusting his chin and food crusting the fur, small brown eyes wide in his face—a pale winter-tanned white—saw him, a giant polar in his way, and tried to barge past anyway.

He grunted and pushed the human back in, and as he did so, caught a brief glimpse of the space beyond.

The door swung shut.

And he waited.

He did not wait long.

His burden opened the door, glided out, and before the door closed once more behind her, he saw things. Stones, tall and grey, hunched over benches, running, cowering, sprawled on the building's rough wood floors, smashed and bleeding.

Grey stone. Bleeding.

He grunted, twisted his head to catch a final glimpse as the door closed, sighing as it found the frame. But he didn't push it open, didn't wedge his paw in the frame and stick his muzzle in for a better look.

His burden had one hand buried in his ruff, her foot in a stirrup and the other hand reaching high for the pommel. She swung on before he could kneel to make it easier, and in so doing, the cloak shifted, the hood falling back an inch, just far enough for one of her thick locks to slip out and hiss.

Red tongue, white mouth, a slit black eye.

She squeezed his giant ribs with her small, bare heels. '*Another*,' she said.

Yes, he thought as he turned and ambled away from the big building with its shit-mixed straw and bleeding rocks in the shape of men. Another.

Bug Hunt

I AM MAGGIE

INTRODUCTION

This story floated in limbo for a while, unsure of its place amongst the other Maggie stories. At first, it competed for space with *Scholar* (Maggie #3), which was a redo of this story, and then it was going to sit where *Felis Fetura* (Maggie #5) is now, but there that thing with the eye in *Felis Fetura,* which felt like it needed an answer.

The eye led to *Vacant Spaces* (Maggie #4), leading to both *Felis Fetura* and *Bug Hunt* getting shunted, and so here we are, at the sixth instalment of *I Am Maggie.*

Despite all the shuffling (and not a little bit of uncertainty about whether or not this was simply a rehash of *Scholar),* I'm happy with how it's all panned out. There is a moment in *Bug Hunt,* started in *Felis Fetura,* that wouldn't have made as much sense if not for *Vacant Spaces.* It's also made the rest of the story start to take shape in my brain; I know who the villain is now.

BUG HUNT

She materialised out of nothing. One moment the world was darkness, an endless void with only the electric-blue glow of the Creation Sphere, the winged avatar floating at its centre, and the next…

The next, an icy mountain wind blew against her cheeks, its frigid fingers playing with the ribbons threaded through her dark, intricate braids – the tiny bells sewn on the ends ringing with sweet melody. It pressed the long ends of her white outer robe against her legs even as it caught in the billowing folds of her greatcoat, the rich, dark-blue fabric flaring behind her like dragon wings.

She lifted her hands and knew them not. The old, knobbled fingers were alien to her, the thick, once-black tattoos a foreign language, their meaning lost somewhere beyond the fuddled edges of her mind, leaving just the knowledge that there was a message in the lines and circles turned green with age. The tattoos covered every inch of pale-gold flesh, from fingertips to palms and wrists, disappearing under her wide, open sleeves.

There was power in that flesh, lined and wrinkled, secrets in her breast—

She pressed a palm to the sudden, piercing ache in her chest and shook her head.

Something was wrong…

An itch on her nape.

She spun, bells jangling in her hair, robes twisting about her legs, greatcoat no longer a dragon's flared wings but mantled like a hawk's.

There was nothing behind her. Nothing save an ocean of dark, polished concrete lit by the setting sun, red and orange lighting up the sky over distant mountains. It bounced off the tops of snow-laden pines and rocky outcrops before spilling through the giant glass wall, long fingers reaching across the cold floor for her feet.

She stepped back—hurriedly—scrunching bare toes tight under skirts and robes, not wanting that yellow-gold light to find her.

And why is that? The thought floated out of the void. Why was she hunkered in this cavernous concrete room, its walls and curved ceiling crawling with ivy? No curtains to black out the searching sun, the end behind her open to wind and rain?

Why?

'Why?' she repeated aloud and was startled at the deep, gravely croak of her own voice. Old, to match her flesh.

Ping! The sound, bright and happy and piercing made her jump, even as a box—a semi-transparent window made of light— appeared in the air before her.

Words scrolled across it, and in the back of her mind, the little voice whispered, 'Dialogue box.'

Dialogue box. Hand to her still-racing heart, Getty closed her eyes and breathed deep. A dialogue box, of course. It was old age playing tricks on her again, that and the Game's mind-bending realism. That'd teach her for getting old, not even two minutes into the Game and she was already losing track.

Silly girl.

Can't let Ben know about this one, the old man would have a fit and then there'd go that sweet monthly check for running her tests. The bonuses too, on those occasions she found a particularly juicy bug, and Lord knew they needed those extra creds filling out their pension.

Especially now.

Getty tapped her still-racing heart.

Most *particularly* now.

Well then... She rubbed old, wizened hands together. 'Time to work,' she said.

The dialogue box hovered in the air at eye height.

// Quest: Bug hunt.

// Reports of faults in the Serenity Bibliotheca causing permanent damage to avatars and user accounts. Locate corrupted items and verify. The devs will not be responsible for loss or damage incurred during the completion of the mission.

// Reward: 500 credits. 3 weeks bonus Game time.

// Bonus mission: Retrieve corrupted artefacts. A quarantine sack has been added to your inventory. Bring corrupted items back for analysis.

// Bonus reward: 2000 credits.

// Accept?

Getty hit the button.

She paused a moment, wide sleeve falling back from her hand—still raised even though the dialogue had winked out of existence—and stared at the faded green dragon tattooed across the back. Had it winked at her?

She shook her head.

No, no, it hadn't. Just her ancient mind playing tricks.

Silly girl, letting old age get the better.

She harrumphed to herself and turned her attention back to the room, her little hidey hole, carved out of the side of a mountain. How could she forget that? All that time, all those experience points and resources, all the side quests and secret missions it had taken to find the right planet, to gather the creds and build the doors.

Honestly, forgetting things like that. Silly girl.

Feet slapping on the dark, chill concrete, long skirts *shushing* behind her, Getty walked to the open window, fingers tracing the wrinkled lines on her left arm as she did so.

Magic shivered under her skin, reaching down through the soles of her feet to the sigils carved into the floor, leaving the bright pop of cherries on her tongue.

Power—bright silver—shot through the charcoal-grey concrete, the cold, sparkling light a perfect match for the snow dusting the mountain pines and the ice on the air. It caught in the lines carved into the window's massive circular edges and shone through the gaps in the vines.

'Poborth Three,' she whispered. 'Serenity Bibliotheca.'

The carvings flashed and, with a great *whomp*, water filled the window – a great, depthless pond replacing the mountain vastness, rippling in an unseen breeze.

Without a pause, Getty stepped into the portal.

The portal was a strange thing, stepping through it stranger still, and though she'd done it many times, somehow this trip felt like the first. The blurred stars, the *whomp whomp whomp* echoing in her bones, the faint aftertaste of cheesecake, the texture of it, the way it clung to the roof of her mouth. Coming out the other side was like coming out of an icy waterfall, a fine layer of frost on her cheeks, weighing down the bells in her hair, settling into her bones.

All those sensations felt new and strange. Alien.

Unlike the Library.

The portal closed, its silver-blue light there one moment, gone the next, leaving her amongst rows of books. Shelves the height of two people stretched above, the warm glow of tulip-shaped lamps shining down. If she stretched her arms wide, she could *almost* touch either side.

Her soles touched the old wood floor—stained a dark, brown-black with age, the boards warped and wobbly—and though she'd never stepped foot among the equally ancient stacks filled with knobbled, leather-bound spines and the dusty scent of actual paper, she knew this place.

It was an electric current that raced over the Tudor-style rafters—more brown-black wood, interspersed with off-white, crumbling plaster—down the shelves and shivered up her calves. She breathed it, felt it, tasted it, saw it on the back of her eyeballs – every page, every scroll and microchip, every ink stain and data bit, welcoming her home.

All of it bar the ugly, itchy niggle behind her ear.

The bug. She knew it like she knew where to find *The Book of Forbidden Knowledge* – fifth edition, the one with the misprinted dedication. After all, she was *the* Scholar, the one, the only, the most powerful, and libraries liked her.

She set off down the aisle, feet a soft thud on the floorboards, the bells in her hair a melodic chime. Strode with enough purpose that her robes—the outer blue and inner white—flared in her wake, dragon wings fluttering over the low wood stools and taller pedestals that lined the aisles.

The itch guided her, turning her right when the first aisle branched, then right and right again. Just when it felt like she was turning back on herself, when she'd surely pop out where she started, it turned her left into a tiny alcove.

There were no shelves here, just a gnarled and knobbled pedestal, the black wood gleaming under the light of a single lamp. On the pedestal, a book. Big enough to need both arms to carry, the cover not made of cloth or leather or even wood, but gold. It lay open, and the pages shone with flecks of the same gold, the ink upon them a deep, rich, midnight shimmering with a hundred colours, as if it were made of black opal.

A trap, if ever she saw one.

Getty huffed. *Noob bait. Of course it's bugged.*

She drew a thin gauze scarf from within her left sleeve, the blue-white material so light it seemed to float, belying the heavy layer of spells woven into the fabric. Everything from protective wards to buffs that boosted her luck, and resistance to physical and magical harm. There was even one that increased her perception, not that she needed it; any higher and pretty soon the virtual world would peel back on itself, exposing its guts for her viewing.

With a practised flick, she wrapped it around her head, covering her eyes. For a heartbeat, the world was the pale blue-white of the scarf, the smells of the Library heightened—the warm mustiness of old paper, the earthier ones of dust and leather—its quiet hush filling her ears, and then a short, bright pulse ran through the scarf and she could see.

See the ridiculous golden book, all but winking at her, come hither practically written all over its opal-inked pages.

She rolled her eyes, double-checked the scarf and stepped fully into the alcove.

The *snap* was subtle, even to her scarf-enhanced perception, the bug's jaws closing behind her.

She scoffed. *Silly bug.* Getty focussed on the book.

The frisson between her shoulder blades and the hint of strawberries on her tongue was her perception digging into the Game's coding. She really shouldn't be able to feel the equations and logic statements *tick ticking* away in the back of her brain, but she was *the* Scholar, and certain stats were so high...

There, right... She twisted her head, crouched a little and...

A squeal. An ugly, nails-on-chalkboard shriek fit to separate her eardrums from her skull accompanied the dialogue that popped to life over the book.

// Scholar Getty:Perception(101). Failure.

What the actual...

...She...

...what?

She scooted closer, as if distance would change the words.

That had to be a mistake.

But no. No matter how she shoved her nose in it, the message didn't change.

She narrowed her gaze, wrapped her long, billowing sleeves

above her elbows, wiry, wrinkled, tattoo-covered forearms exposed to the world, and focussed harder.

No glittery noob-bait book was getting the better of her.

Again the frisson, the strawberries, the *tick ticking*.

For the longest time, nothing happened, then...

The words scattered, letters peeling away from letters, punctuation marks flying left, paragraphs right, even the pages themselves... Getty closed her eyes, swaying on her feet, the floorboards no longer feeling quite as level, the bookshelf not as straight. A hand reaching out, the warm smoothness of wood, the rough touch of cloth-bound covers.

A deep breath, bringing with it the rich, musty scent of old paper and the new, colder smell of micro-pages and the hum of electronics.

She could do this.

This was what she'd rolled for, why she'd sacrificed charm and strength for intelligence and logic. Why she was standing here, Brother Thoth's old, tattered robes beneath her over-tunic and greatcoat, the hem playing with her knees, her toes tracing every bump and divot in the floor. Why she'd chosen monk as her profession all those decades ago. Had it really been decades? It seemed like mere moments since she'd run through Uxen Prime.

..

Getty shook herself, regathered her scattered thoughts.

Now wasn't the time for wool-gathering, Ben would be back before she knew it, and there was that neat little wave cooker she'd seen on the infomercials... and the medical bills...

Focus, Getty. Focus.

A deep breath, rolling her shoulders, shifting her stance on the floorboards. A little wider, a little more settled. She could do this.

She *focused*. A narrowing of gaze, a twitch of her eyelashes and...

// Sister Getty:Perception(120). Success.

// Ancient Scroll unlocked.

Victory lent an extra thump to her heart, but she didn't let it distract her. This was just the beginning. If the books in the Library were bugged, then just reading them was the start of it. Whatever was wrong, would be in the reading.

'[Ghostly Sight],' she whispered.

A pulse, and a faint hum filled her ears even as a film clouded her vision, just a moment of fuzzy whiteness before the fine strip of milky, gauze-like material settled over eyes and ears, and the spells in it came to life. Whatever dangers might lie between the pages, [Ghostly Sight] would catch them before they did her any real harm.

If she was lucky.

She flipped the page, the new-ancient parchment thick and heavy between her tattooed fingers, the microcircuits embedded between the fibres still icy. On it, the ink paused, the words and paragraphs rearranging themselves into ordered lines of spiky, quill-inked text, merely vibrating now—shaking like the cold under her feet was making their teeth chatter too—instead of the crazy dance of before. But still... the meaning behind them...

Getty leaned closer. Closer still. Until her nose almost touched the parchment. It smelled of dust, and something else. Something old and musty but with a sooty edge, the remains of an ancient fire, but the words...

It was a Latin alphabet; round swoops and dashing lines of 'bs' and 'ks' easy to pick out, but the way the letters were arranged was strange. It tickled the back of her head and made her think of deep, dark dungeons and planets once discovered but now forgotten. Was it part of the bug? A cipher perhaps?

Getty straightened, frowning now. She'd been studying it long enough, her knowledge banks should have already pinged or [Ghostly Sight] sprung a warning, as it was...

An Intelligence check this time, augmented by the Esoteric Languages trait in her Ability tree.

// Sister Getty:Intelligence:Esoteric Languages(40). Success.

A translucent dialogue popped over the scroll.

// 907(|-|4, |\/|49913.

What the fuck? That wasn't even—

She flipped the page.

The dialogue changed with it. More gobbledegook filling the translucent window.

Another flip.

More nonsense words.

What the hell was—

Red soaked her vision.

A new dialogue superimposed itself over the first. [Ghostly Sight] doing its work.

// Virus detected.

The victory she'd suppressed flooded back.

'Got you,' she whispered, and then, to the System. '[Tag].'

// Location tagged. Bug reported.

// Quest: Bug Hunt. Success. Congratulations, Sister Ge- Ge- Ge-GGGGGGG...

The victory turned cold.

// System error 57. Unspecified. Please contact your network administrat— administrat— administrat—

Text scrolled across the dialogue, filling the translucent window and then spilling over the edge. The words bled over the sides and into the world, turning liquid as they did, each letter a milky raindrop soaking her over-robe.

Getty stumbled back, and the drops broke on the floorboards instead, pooling on the dark floor.

The victory was dust on her tongue. No, not just dust, but foul pore-clogging ashes, thick and sooty, gumming up her tastebuds, stuck in her nose, creeping down her throat with the gooey, slimy chill of ghoul flesh.

She stared at the puddle, growing larger, at the words still spilling over the dialogue's edge, and just... just...

A moment.

Another.

The puddle hit the base of the plinth and parted, the milky pool lapping at the old wood before spreading fingers either side.

She watched it. Knew in the back of her mind that she should do something, [Tag] it or hit [Record] or dig the black quill out of her bag and open a window into the Debug, but... but...

She stood there. Stupid and dumb, frozen to the spot like someone had grabbed hold of all her reason and pressed [Pause].

The words continued to spill—*splish splish splish*—and the puddle grew until soon enough, it formed a little moat. A moat that, instead of spreading outward, began to climb. Five long, thin streams flowing up, twisting around the wood like fingers... Fingers that thickened at the base, joining to form a palm and then a wrist and forearm...

The thing holding Getty to the spot cracked, its icy shards slipping through her blood. She backed up, the wood warm compared to the chill emanating from the hand reaching out of that puddle.

It had an elbow now, and its sinewy fingers were wrapped around the gnarly knob midway up the plinth's stem. Tendons and veins stood out over the back of it, corded muscles in the forearm, and it *pulled*, lifting more of itself out of the milky pond.

Words continued to spill from the dialogue box, and on the book...

The unintelligible string of lines and dots began to move again. Faster and faster as the hand crawled upward, milky nails leaving crescent marks in the wood. Sharp lines twisted and writhed, slipping one over the other in a crosshatch, multiplying until a shape lifted its head from the parchment.

Long and pointed, with blazing eyes and gnarled tree branches for horns.

A dragon coiled on the page.

It blinked at her. Flicked its long, forked tongue and hissed.

She stared back at it.

Hurry, it seemed to say. *Hurry. Hurry.*

And just like that, something clicked in the back of her skull, the foggy haze of age lifted and for one shiny moment everything was clear. Who she was, how she was, what she needed to do.

So clear, so bright, so... so...

Gone.

Gone except for the quill in her pocket, the hard piercing tip digging through the Robes of Thoth to draw blood from her thigh.

Blood to write with.

Blood to reveal.

Blood to banish the thing pulling itself out of the milky puddle.

But not here, she needed... she needed...

Silly girl. It had been right there, right on the tip of her brain. How could she forget?

The hand wasn't just a hand anymore, or an elbow. There was a shoulder, a neck, an ear, the back of a head. A second hand. *Thwack* against the boards, pushing even as the first gripped the edge of the plinth and pulled.

The dragon hissed again.

Go, it said.

Getty ran.

And ran and ran and ran. Bare soles smacked the floor, robes streaming behind, the cold biting her nose even as exertion flushed her cheeks and adrenaline powered her heart.

Her endurance bar ran low.

Faded.

Died.

She gasped, dust hitting the back of her throat, lungs burning, a stitch like a knife ripping her side.

Why was she running? What was she—?

Hand in her pocket, pain against her palm.

The quill. The blood. She glanced behind, down the endless lines of shelves, the books and side tables, imagining she could see around the corners, the gaps between bookcases, the backs of chairs, to the plinth and the dragon and the thing...

The thing.

The thing to banish.

With the quill.

With the blood.

Her blood.

A scholar's blood.

A scholar's power.

A scholar's knowledge.

The age-fog parted.

Another heartbeat of clarity.

She straightened.

A book. She needed a book. But not any book, the *right* book. A hidden book, with a hidden purpose. An Easter Egg.

The quill sang as it came out of her pocket – a single high, pure note.

The midnight feathers rippled a thousand colours—purple, blue, red and violet—and the ink-dark tip glistened.

Getty narrowed her gaze and focussed on that shiny drop, the way it budded on the sharp tip, how the quill's very blackness seemed to draw all colour from it. How it hung, sticky and viscous. Waiting.

In the back of her mind, the System buzzed. Variables slotted into algorithms, formulas rushing through servers, hitting logic loops. Avatar stats stacked—Intelligence and Perception—pitted against Luck and the ever-present god of the random number generator, to determine the outcome of her actions. Some said the Game was all numbers, that no matter how immersive the experience, how real the wind, how convincing the cakes and pies and pain, that the player's will had no effect on the outcome. Others weren't quite so sure.

Getty focused. Focused hard. She believed. Believed hard. She wasn't just a scholar, she was *the* Scholar. All brain and no brawn. She'd faced down Library ghouls and retrieved lost artefacts with nothing but a scroll and her own wit. Age might have wrinkled her skin and buzzed her recall, but it couldn't take the power in her mind, the strength of her intellect, the inevitability of her single-minded focus.

With the quill in her grasp, the Game was hers, whether the System realised that or not.

'Show me the book,' she said, the command falling like bells.

The *click* echoed; a deep vibration like the Game itself snapped its fingers.

But it wasn't paper or papyrus, parchment or vellum that hovered in the air, wasn't even a book or the green and black wireframe of the Debug. For a second, despite the System *ping*, Getty thought she'd done it wrong, that age had muddled her memory of the commands, had robbed her of the correct intonation, the precise flourish of quill in space. At the very least, there should have been a cursor, a dialogue, a map, a pixie or arrow or team of wild rabbits springing out of the wood to show her the way, to show her the *thing*. Instead... instead the air shimmered, and what appeared in front of her was... her.

Sister Getty, aged and wrinkled, a short, straight scarecrow adorned in blue and white robes, bells and ribbons in her long, dark hair, tattoos creeping over her hands. She stared at the illusion of herself, at the row of monstrous shelves, the dimly lit tables and plinths visible through her translucent form, and wondered if maybe Ben was right. Did too old to drive really mean too old to surf?

She was not the Easter Egg, she was—

The tattoos on illusion-Getty's hands shone a brilliant white.

The tattoos, the secrets written on her skin.

Of course.

Silly girl.

Getty raised her hands. She was *the* Scholar after all. What need did she have of the ink in books when she carried it on her skin?

In the distance, through the hazy illusion of herself, a figure moved. Tall and twisted and milky, *slosh sloshing* its way down the corridor.

There was a breeze behind it, carrying the putrid stench of old water. Dust and rot mixed together.

It wailed; a high, melodic sound that nonetheless sent shivers down her spine, made the flesh stand up on the back of her neck and sent chill water through her veins. It wailed on. The sound bounced off the shelves and rattled the glass domes over the artefacts.

Getty steeled herself, shoved the shivers and the chills aside and turned her Perception on the thing coming down the corridor.

A ping. A new dialogue, wobbly and distorted. Text turned to gobbledegook.

She hissed, fisted her hands and shifted her bare feet. Whatever virus or worm this thing was, it was powerful and entrenched in the System if just looking at it could mess with the interface. It needed a dev, not a bug hunter.

But still... she was *the* Scholar, and no bug would get the better of her.

'[Ghostly Sight],' she whispered.

// Sister Getty:Ghostly Sight(79) vs |)|_||_70n:Magic resist(30). Success.

The dialogue box steadied, the cross-hatched lines and squares rearranging themselves into an alphabet she recognised.

// Revenant. Level 89. The spirit of a legendary warrior long since dead. WARNING: System error. NPC class in beta. Do not interact. Do not scan. Do not—

The rest of it was cut off, but Getty didn't need more.

A revenant was nothing. She could deal with a—

The wail hit again. No longer just a sound raising gooseflesh but a force, a silver shimmer in the air rocketing down the narrow aisle, picking up dust and debris, and slamming into her chest.

Getty stumbled, pushed backward by the violent force, robes blowing out behind, hair and ribbons billowing, bells *clanging*, the sound too loud and too deep for such tiny instruments. A warning. Like the colour soaking the veil, no longer red but a deep, bloody crimson-black.

She gripped the quill hard, fighting against the foul gale trying to hold her arms against her sides and encapsulate her legs, to prevent her from raising her hand.

The wail grew with every micron, every muscle twitch, and Getty's teeth were locked, her jaw screaming by the time she brought it around, and then, when the pointed black end was hovering over her skin—

Smack.

A magnet slamming the tip into the back of her hand, hard enough she felt it in her bones, pain ricocheting up her arm, stealing the life from her elbow. And then another fight to draw the quill out. Once she did... not blood that streamed from her hand to the quill but grey-green ink, flowing from her tattoos like a river in reverse.

Pain and effort creased Getty's brow, made sweat pop on her nape and that sick-hungry sensation to boil her, but it didn't dim her smile, didn't blunt the hard edge of it.

Another ear-shredding wail, another wave of stench-rot, another *shlop shlop* as the revenant oozed down the aisle, pushing Getty back. It seemed to draw the colour out of the Library as it went, absorbed the bright pops of green and red and royal blue from the covers, the deep mahogany from the shelves. And as it did... images danced across the thing's milky chest, like an old-fashioned projector against a worn screen in a too-light room. The images caught at Getty's eyes, drew her attention away from the quill, the ink...

A basement. A dark-skinned woman tied to a metal chair. Another woman in an old pleather recliner, the kind she remembered seeing in history vids. A man, tall and skinny like the revenant, turned away from the camera...

Rank water filled her nose, the musty scent creeping over her tongue. Damp, putrid breath on her face—

Getty jerked backward, alarm making her clumsy, heels catching in her robes, and almost putting her on her backside.

The revenant's face just a metre from hers, its milky, melted features shifting, ears melting into neck, nose into lips, eyes first big and round then small and oblong.

Another jerk back, quill coming back up from where it had fallen to her side, ink still streaming from her hand to the nib.

Colour still shifted under the revenant's liquid skin, trying to suck her back in. Getty planted her feet, embraced the ice creeping up her soles, and wrote.

Letters danced from the quill, the grey-green sinking into the air like there was some kind of invisible parchment soaking up the ink. After fire, they bled, edges blurring, the words indistinct, and the quill fought her, wanted to skid left then right, up then down, but she gritted her teeth and held on.

The revenant advanced, even as the first word took shape.

"Bind."

She completed the word with a flourish, and as if it was the key, the quill's resistance eased, the next letter and the next word coming easier and faster until the tip was flashing through space, sharp, grey-green words burning.

"Banish."

The revenant screeched and lurched forward, its watery hands outstretched, fingers hooked.

"End."

The revenant juddered to a stop, arms and half its torso bursting through the words. The green-grey ink wrapped around its body "bind" and "banish" and "end" twisting around its ribs. The monster strained, the words stretching, vowels growing longer and fatter, distorting almost beyond recognition. Almost, but not quite, not enough to break the text.

Putrid white nails flexed, the tips millimetres from her face, the stench entrenching itself in her brain. Never to be forgotten.

The toothless mouth stretched wide, a yawning hole in the shifting, liquid face. Before it could wail, Getty lifted the quill and with the last of the ink on her skin, finished the paragraph with a final dot.

For a second, nothing happened and then... the monster collapsed, not to its knees or hands like a living thing, but like a water-filled balloon – straight down, no form no grace, just a murky, milky puddle spreading over the dark wood.

The last thing to go was the thing's face, the blurred, shifting features melting into the puddle. The last thing was its lips, the thin, pale skin parting around a final word. 'Maa-ggieeee,' it said, and then was gone.

The Deli

INTRODUCTION

I used to work in the deli section at the local supermarket, which was terrible because it was so very boring (spoiler: bored authors are dangerous). However, there were a few upsides, this story being one.

I don't know exactly how the idea came about, but while I was cleaning the cabinets, I started imagining a magical version of the deli. What kind of things would it serve? Who would the customers be? Would everyone know the deli was magic? And what *exactly* made it magic?

Well, first things first, be it a real deli or a magical one, time works differently when you're behind the counter—five minutes feels like twenty—so I started there.

Our deli had crappy lino flooring (which was actually pretty good lino flooring, considering the abuse it got) that, in my brain, somehow transformed itself in marble tiles soaked in magical wards, and the rest went from there.

THE DELI

Time moves differently in the Deli. Sometimes fast, sometimes slow. Never the same for each person, even if they're standing on the same marble tile.

Some say it's the centuries of spells laid into the foundations, the generations of wizards and sorcerers, the witches, djinns and hedge mages, the demigods and legendaries leaving little pieces of themselves behind with every footfall across the hallowed ground. Others, that the ancient powers who made this place, who laid the spells along with the foundations, the wards with the mortar, the blessings with the beams, used the last of their godly powers to makes the place live. Others still, that it was an accident, that the warp is the leftover of some terrible battle, a tear in the forces of nature. That those who venture behind the counters and into the storerooms beyond the great kitchen, are lost in that tear. That only they know the secrets hidden in the bricks and mortar.

The only truth is that the Deli exists. Its tiny, glass-fronted store never where you expect it, but always where you need it. On a busy city street, in the darkest corner of the meanest neighbourhood, buried in a cliff-face, hidden under a tent. On a boat. Under the sea. The Deli finds you, wherever you are, the rich scent of sausage, honeyed baklava, spiced terrine or warm quiche calling to you from between Christmas shoppers, down alleys or through war-zones. Whatever smell reminds you the most of home, safety or revenge, reaches out and hooks itself in your nose and pulls you along.

You can't escape it even if you know what it is, what it wants, or what you think it wants.

No one's ever been able to figure that out either—what the Deli wants—another mystery hidden in the grey-white marble floors, the shiny counter tops and glittering refrigerator fronts. All the scholars can agree on is that it *does* want something, that there is some grand design, a rhyme and reason to the people it draws through its doors.

Most come once and leave, a parcel wrapped in brown paper in their hands, never noticing the brown string dangling from their thumb or tied around their ankle. Sometimes, the strings are long, other times they are short. But the people leave, disappear into whatever arcade or desert or war they wandered in from, completely unaware of the magic they just touched.

Those people never come back.

The ones that do come back drip power like the spits drip meat juices, hissing and sizzling on coals that never go out. The witches and wizards, necromancers and elves, paladins and knights of old, the ones who know where to look, how to want, how to *use*. The kind of beings the Deli likes to embroil in its grand plans, whatever that might be.

They are the ones who slink through the door and capture the light, or shadows as the case may be. I sometimes think the Deli caters to them, repositions the spotlights just so, adjusts the crystals in the window, manipulates shadow and sunlight like a Las Vegas casino host drawing in a whale. The powerful ones lap it up. Pause just that moment in the spectacle, like we don't know they're there, like we haven't been expecting them. Like the Deli hasn't told us.

Like we aren't the ones with the real power.

N

Time moves differently for each thing and each person, like the legendary and the... I tilt my head to the side, taking in the fawn-coloured tweed jacket and the loafers peeking from under the navy moleskin trousers. Old-fashioned Oxford university professor, if my education in pre-millennium pop culture was anything to go by.

Which it was. I've studied hard after all, and if the professor wasn't an updated clone of a certain vampire slayer's librarian mentor, I was handing in my certificate.

Or my apron. Goddess, I really need to hand in my apron. The checked navy cotton has an egg stain on the breast and what feels like half a litre of olive oil soaked into the hem, along with the juices from the chickens in the big roaster. Enough of both to have soaked through my overskirt and leave an unpleasant wet patch on my petticoat. Plus, there was at least one old price sticker stuck on my back by Mirelle and three more on my shirt breast, just above my corset.

Magic hums through each: three wards, one blessing and... I wriggle my shoulder blades... A good luck charm.

Mirelle should have kept it for herself, maybe then she'd be serving the professor instead of stuck with the legendary.

Both legendary and professor are contemplating the offerings in the salad cabinet; beetroot and carrot, creamy pasty, and egg side-by-side with tabbouleh, fattoush and kachumber, among others. The professor leans in close to the glass and I wonder just how much he needs the wireframe spectacles sliding down his hawk-like nose, and just how long he spent choosing the navy tie to go with his dove-grey shirt. The whole outfit seems a little bit too much to be true, polished much like the Deli's grey-white marble tiles and plate-glass windows.

Slick.

Shiny.

Not as shiny as the legendary's armour though. Erneada is her usual resplendent self in her gold-chased silver breastplate and greaves; long, white-silk cape flowing from her pauldrons, blonde curls falling over both, and the Deli is loving her for it.

A quarter candle-mark before the mage-knight threw open the doors, the Deli switched the overhead fluros out for a wagon-wheel candelabra, complete with foot-long waxy stalactites. There were even sconces on the walls behind and the lights in the cabinets were no longer a cold blue-white but a buttery-warm flicker. The perfect lighting for the tall, elegant woman with her refined air and so much magic in her bones the air sparkles around her.

She is one of the Deli's favourites and it's slowed time to keep her a little longer. The magic motes twinkle like drunk stars around her head—slow and sleepy—and she's been frowning at the Thai beef salad longer than the anaemic lettuce and stringy beef require. Probably wondering why the coriander is wilting before her eyes.

Not so much the professor.

The middle-aged man with his greying, tousled hair, three-day beard and the tomato sauce stain on his collar is in real time. Or, at least, my time.

Mirelle, standing beside me with her pasted-on smile and hands folded at her waist—lest she start drumming her fingers on the cabinet—is stuck in Erneada's space, moving with the same liquid slowness as the mage-knight, but unlike the mage-knight, she's aware of the difference. Painfully aware.

There's going to be hell to pay later.

But not a problem for now.

I brighten my smile and lean a little into the counter-top, projecting charisma through the refrigerated cabinet. The magic is half test, half a desperate wish to hurry him through his purchase and out the door. If he can see the rainbow shimmer (doubtful) he's not who he's pretending to be and if he can't… My shift was meant to end eight minutes ago, precisely one minute after he wandered in off whatever cobblestoned laneway he called home. The faster I get him out of here, the faster *I* go home.

'We have a lovely Brussel sprout salad with apples and walnuts today, sir, if you'd like to try it.' My lips are going to fall off and my cheekbones hurt from smiling for three days straight, the length of my current shift. It's going to take the whole week to unfreeze my muscles and twice that long to undo the psychological damage of having to be nice and *social.*

The professor "hmmms" and pushes his glasses back up his nose. He keeps peering into the cabinet. The same cabinet he's been peering into for the last six minutes. Really, there's not that much in there, and nothing that warrants the hawk-eyed inspection.

I clasp my hands behind my back, squeezing them tight just like Mirelle's doing, lest my fingers *tap tap tap* on the serving board.

'We also have a butternut squash and freekeh—'

He looks up; a sudden, quick movement, and it takes all my century of experience behind the counter not to flinch at the look in his eyes. Hard, sharp, a molten spear aimed at my brain. 'Do you have pies?'

I blink. 'Pies?' *Not a professor*, is all I can think. Totally not a professor. Not quite enough power in the gold-brown orbs for a demi-god through, and not the right flavour for a high wizard. Necromancer perhaps, or a half-djinn?

He nods, and I wonder if it's because he's slipped through my mental shields or if he's still on the pies. 'Or maybe a quiche? Vegetarian.'

I nod. 'Over here.' I gesture to the cabinet on Mirelle's other side even as I slip around her. For a heartbeat, I'm caught in her time warp, the air becoming thick and heavy, gravity hugging my feet a little tighter, sound a thick syrup, and then I'm out.

One sixth time; I can tell from the way my skin crawls coming out of it. Fuck, I'm glad of the blessing Mirelle slapped on my back, the woman herself is gonna be stuck in there for hours, maybe even a day unless the mage-knight picks up her pace.

The hell gate in the third under-basement opening a decade ahead of schedule was more likely, but stranger things had happened. It was the Deli, after all, and even we don't know exactly what it's planning.

A bit like the not-professor, hunched over and now peering into the pastry cabinet, a little frown between his brows. He's kinda hot in his academic tweediness, what with that unexpected hint of power, but the hotness doesn't stop me wanting to bounce on my sensibly shod heels and wish he'd hurry the fuck up.

I have a date with a labyrinth and a pizza, and he's making me late.

He points a finger with the kind of callouses you don't get from wielding a pen, at a palm-sized, blood-red quiche layered with thin slices of broccoli at the back. The crust is pale gold—*actual* gold, not blonde—and the filling sparkles under the cold cabinet lights.

'Does it have egg?' He looks up from under his glasses, and those eyes... Still a gut-shot and too hot for a necromancer, literally. The half-djinn is seeming more likely, and probably just out of the aether, hence the pop culture professor.

I nod. 'Dragon.'

He echoes my nod, points at the blue quiche beside the dragon-egg one. 'And this?'

The pastry encasing the mermaid quiche is a dark chocolate, and if you look at it sideways, you can almost see waves surging through the seaweed and squid ink filling. 'No egg, and the ink is farmed.'

Another nod, and for a second his eyes flick between the two, and—hit me with a brick—if he isn't actually *melting* the glass front.

At least I'm not on the clean-up shift tonight.

He taps the glass. 'I'll take the red one. Can you heat it for me?'

'It's self-heated,' I say as I grab a to-go carton from under the counter and tongs from the jug beside the cabinet, careful to select the ones with the red handles. The cabinet door slides open as I lean in, the smell of brimstone and sea salt immediately fighting for attention. 'Just the one?'

Another nod. He pushes his glasses up his nose again. 'But maybe also one of those little cakes with the…' And he sticks up that oddly calloused finger and twirls it.

'The horn. Sure, just let me pop the lid on this.'

'No rush,' he says.

I don't snort. I want to, just like I want to stomp my sensibly-shod feet, snap my skirts and snarl, but I don't. He might not be in a rush, but there's a pizza calling my name.

I box the quiche and scoot over to the dessert cabinet to do the same for the Unicorn tart in record time. The tart sings as I close little pearl-handled tongs around the base—a pale gold to match the blood quiche—emitting a burst of raspberry sparkles. It goes in its own box—best not to mix the two, if only so the hell gate in the third under-basement doesn't get any ideas—and slide them over the top of the glass cabinet.

The professor watches me the entire way. I know because those molten eyes have left welts on the back of my hands.

Unexpected. And a little concerning.

Definitely something with a little more oomph than a half-djinn. An actual *dragon* perhaps?

I can't help but pale a little at the thought and slide a glance at Erneada in her shiny armour, white cape and long blonde curls. You can't see it, but there's a greatsword strapped to the mage-knight's back, a double-handed affair with a blackened steel hilt at odds with the knight's silver and gold-chased armour.

I've only ever laid eyes on it once, and never the blade itself, but the crescent-shaped guard with the blue stone in its centre is hard to forget, if only because of the way it screams.

It's the kind of sound that climbs through your earbuds all the way to your soul. Madness and terror all mixed up until you can't be sure if the madness came before the terror or the terror before the mad. In the end, it doesn't matter because you're curled up on the floor with your fingers in your eyeballs.

Or at least, that's what happens to the norms, the Deli looks after its staff. Hard to find replacements and all.

Right now though, that's the least of my worries, because Erneada's sword has a certain reputation, and if the pop culture professor is what I fear…

Best to wrap this up quick.

I meet those molten eyes—do they glow hotter now and are those scales peeking through his hairline?—and smile. 'Will there be anything else?'

He smiles back, and yes, that is a fang pressing into his lower lip. 'A haunch of dragon-slayer, if you have any.'

Well, fuck.

Slowly, I reach under the countertop, index finger searching for the little Celtic knot carved in the underside, even as I widen my smile. 'I'm sorry, the Deli doesn't stock sentient meats, but we do have a lovely leg of miniature rock wyvern, if you're interested.'

Please, don't be interested.

Please ignore the screaming, greatsword-wielding dragon-slayer on the hoof, caught in a convenient time warp just a metre to your right. At least until I can find that fucking emergency knot.

Please. Pretty, pretty please with the Unicorn tart on top.

The not-professor's smile widens as his mouth elongates and the scales at his hairline creep over his forehead. His gaze turns to molten lead, and the good luck charm on my back shrivels up and turns to dust.

I know, because I can smell it, clover and shit wafting over my shoulder.

Why can I never find the emergency knot when I need it?

'What about that one?' The professor points at Erneada, the nails on his oddly calloused hand no longer pale human nails but thick black talons. And it's not like he needs me to answer, not like he doesn't already know the mage-knight's a slayer, any more than I need to know that he's playing with me. Because he's a dragon, and dragons are arseholes.

And you know what? The minute hand on the big ol' clock over the door is pointing at thirteen past the hour, and that's thirteen fucking minutes for my pizza to get cold, and I've had enough of this shit.

The smile drops from my lips and I know my eyes have changed colour by the way the professor/dragon blinks and from the new, heady fear scent washing away the busted charm. My eyes are just the first change, the rest forces the dragon back a step, and then another.

By the time the halos outlining my new long, serpent-like tresses and my horns are flirting with the roof beams, he's busting arse – out the front door, quiche and tart orphaned on the glass cabinet top, hightailing it down whatever cobblestoned street he calls home.

Yeah arsehole, you better run.

I shrink back to my regular size, shucking the apron as I do and swiping the quiche and Unicorn tart from the cabinet top. Spoils from the recent battle.

Beside me at the salad cabinet, Mirelle's frowning, and I know she's seen it all, even if the mage-knight is oblivious to her near-death experience.

When my boss finds out I revealed my true form to a customer, she's going to throw a fit, but the need for subtlety passed the moment the professor started sprouting scales, and if the boss doesn't agree… Well, she knows where to find me.

After my date with a pizza.

ACKNOWLEDGMENTS

Acknowledgments are a funny thing. After five volumes of Short Bits (plus all those other books), you'd think they'd get easier to write, but no, no they don't. So I'm gonna do it differently this time, and dedicate this section to the thirty fabulous heroes who supported the *Short Bits Volume 5 Kickstarter*. You Rebels brought the Limited Special Edition* to life and helped shape these tales of defiance across the multiverse. I hope you love it.

These Destiny Defiers are: Billye Herndon, Amanda Escjm, Michael Lasco, Scruffy Bear, Cat Gardiner, chesscommands, Mike Dobey, Ian Chung, Kelly McMahon, K.R.S., Iris Juylyenne, Joe Lau, Meyari McFarland, Nicolas Lobotsky, Dead Fish Books, Patrick Hay, Ashley Allison, António Matos, Jessica Cline, asakunotomohiro, Arend van 't Oever, David Holzborn and Kristen Altmann.

*If the copy in your hands isn't the Limited Special Edition… you missed something special. The special edition was strictly limited to the Kickstarter campaign and is no longer available. If you want to get in on the rebellion, make sure to join the mailing list so you don't miss the next limited edition!

DON'T MISS
ANOTHER BOOK!

I love keeping in touch with my readers, it's the second-best thing about being a writer (writing being the first best). Every fortnight (or thereabouts), I send out a newsletter with details about upcoming offers, new releases and extra special projects.

If you sign up for the mailing you'll receive exclusive behind-the-scenes extras, such as:

- free short stories
- deleted and alternate scenes from my books
- previews of upcoming books
- pancakes
- quizes
- and much, much more!

Scan the QR code or visit the link below to sign up.
belindacrawford.com/newsletter

READY FOR MORE?

**A gritty, action-packed thriller
served with a chilling side of revenge.**

Vlad – gamer, hacker, scourge… Angel of Death.

Vlad's parents died in a car accident; she can still feel the flames licking her skin, smell the burning batteries and fire-retardant. Except it wasn't an accident, someone made it happen.

She's has spent the last nine years tracking those responsible; planning, plotting.

She's almost done.

When the last move is over, her opponent will wish they never played with the Angel of Death.

Available now
belindacrawford.com/Gamer

ABOUT THE AUTHOR

Physics makes Belinda's brain hurt, while quadratics cause her eyes to cross and any mention of probability equations will have her running for the door. Nonetheless, she loves watching documentaries about the natural world, biology, space, history and technology.

She's also a sucker for a fast horse, a faster computer and superhero movies. When she's not doing the horse, computer or superhero thing, Belinda writes sci-fi and fantasy for readers who like their fiction action-packed, with diverse characters, butt-kicking heroines and complex worlds.

As a certified crazy horse person, when she's not wrangling six-legged dynamos on the page, she's wrangling four-legged powder-kegs in the paddock. Belinda brings that same certified craziness to her writing with the kind of unexpected twists that'll keep you guessing.

You can keep in touch with Belinda, or just pick her brains about sci-fi via her website, Facebook or by sending her an email (she loves email).

www.belindacrawford.com
belinda@belindacrawford.com

Have news delivered straight to your inbox
via her mailing list. Sign up at:
belindacrawford.com/newsletter

www.ingramcontent.com/pod-product-compliance
Lightning Source LLC
Chambersburg PA
CBHW020533120726
47904CB00003B/1057